< Jean Slaughter Doty >

THE VALLEY
OF THE PONIES

Illustrated by Dorothy Haskell Chhuy

MACMILLAN PUBLISHING CO., INC.
New York
COLLIER MACMILLAN PUBLISHERS
London

Copyright © 1982 Jean Slaughter Doty
Copyright © 1982 Macmillan Publishing Co., Inc.

All rights reserved. No part of this book may be reproduced or transmitted in any form or by any means, electronic or mechanical, including photocopying, recording or by any information storage and retrieval system, without permission in writing from the Publisher.

Macmillan Publishing Co., Inc.
866 Third Avenue, New York, N.Y. 10022
Collier Macmillan Canada, Ltd.

Printed in the United States of America

10   9   8   7   6   5   4   3   2   1

Library of Congress Cataloging in Publication Data
Doty, Jean Slaughter, date.
The valley of the ponies.
Summary: Jennifer's wonderful summer with a pony of her own is marred by a tense encounter with horse thieves.
[1. Ponies—Fiction.   2. Crime and criminals—Fiction]   I. Chhuy, Dorothy Haskell, ill.
II. Title.
PZ7.D7378Val   [Fic]   81–19381
ISBN 0–02–732790–6   AACR2

To
Honey Bee
and to
Chanelle—
good ponies. Though they've
known this, themselves, all along.

<1>

The sagging old cow barn was streaky with faded red paint. The black pony I was trying to lead inside didn't like it at all. Tired as she was after her long trip in the trailer, Melissa snorted and fussed and shook her mane disgustedly as I tried to coax her through the door.

"Behave yourself, Melissa," I said to her crossly. I was tired, too. Some of my hair had escaped from its pony-tail and was flopping in my face, which always drove me crazy. Melissa was giving me a hard time, and depressing gray clouds were piling up over the tops of the trees, with the wind promising rain.

Maybe having a pony for the summer hadn't been such a good idea, after all. I was nervous; I'd never taken care of a pony completely by myself before. I decided unhappily that I didn't know nearly enough about it.

Melissa yanked at her lead rope. All the gray gloom outside didn't help the looks of the inside of the cow barn. But I knew, even if the pony didn't, that there was a nice stall inside—not a fancy one, but it was big, and deep in fresh, sweet bedding that I'd put there myself before getting Melissa off the trailer. I'd hung a fresh

1

bucket of water in one corner and a rubber feed tub in another. The tub wasn't hung very straight, but I didn't think the pony would mind.

Melissa tiptoed into the stall, pawed suspiciously at the shavings, and flopped down to roll in them with a contented sigh. I dashed out the door to get out of the way, then turned to watch her as she waved her hoofs in the air. When she got up she was covered in shavings, but she looked a lot calmer. She shook herself, drank a few sips of water, and went over to bury her muzzle in the pile of sweet hay I'd put in the corner of her stall.

"Everything will look better in the morning," I said to the pony, just as Mom had said to me as we'd wearily started to unpack the station wagon and the trailer. I shoved the stall door shut and latched it. A gust of wind blew a sprinkle of rain on my face, and it was pouring by the time I'd made sure everything was snug and tight.

Even though it wasn't very late, it was getting dark. Outside the barn, the horse trailer sagged against the hitch on the back of the station wagon. But the light in the window of the house across the yard shone golden and welcoming.

"I'll come back after supper," I shouted to Melissa. Ducking my head against the rain, I raced toward the house.

Mom and Dad were in the kitchen tripping over stacks of packing boxes. There was a teakettle chirping to itself on the back of the stove and the wonderful smell of cooking things from a fat orange pot.

Dad was on his hands and knees looking for an electric outlet so he could plug in the refrigerator. The teakettle boiled over, bubbling a gush of water from its spout. Mom waved one hand toward a jumble of boxes near the door.

"Your things are in there," she said, diving for the kettle. "You'd better change your clothes—you're soaked! Your room's right at the top of the stairs on the left. There's no light yet in the hall, I think the bulb's burned out, but I left a lamp on in your room. . . ."

While she rummaged in a basket for a potholder, I found a boxful of jeans and sweaters and staggered upstairs with the carton in my arms.

I liked my room. It was small and the ceiling sloped at funny angles, but there was plenty of room for a brass bed and a small chest of drawers, and there was a bathroom right next to it. The back window of the room looked out over the cow barn and a dim, blank smear of light behind it. That must be the pasture behind the barn.

The room was damp and stuffy and cold. The house hadn't been used all winter. But Dad had brought up a small electric heater and it was gallantly puffing little breaths of heat out into the room. I didn't know what to do with all my wet clothes, so I just dumped them on the floor of the bathroom, found a pair of heavy corduroys and a thick sweater in the box of my stuff, and pulled them on. I hurried back down the stairs, tugging a comb through my wet hair. I'd make up my bed later, when the room was warmer.

Mom was looking tired and frantic. Dad was still groping with the refrigerator cord on his hands and knees. Rain splattered on the kitchen window.

"Welcome to the sweet New England summer," Dad said in a muffled voice. The teakettle boiled over again and everybody laughed. If we hadn't, we'd have all sat down and cried because we were so tired. But it wasn't long before we found plates and knives and forks, and a loaf of bread and some butter. Mom had brought a whole cooler full of good things in the back of the station wagon, and I don't know when I've ever tasted anything better than the supper that first cold night of the summer.

Feeling warm at last and a lot more cheerful, we sat dreamily at the round kitchen table. Mom and Dad sipped their coffee and I had a mugful of cocoa—we'd forgotten to bring marshmallows, but, for a change, I didn't even care. I hooked my bare toes over the rung of my chair, wondered lazily if I'd seen any socks in the box upstairs, and decided I was too warm and sleepy to go to look for them.

< 2 >

"That's better," Dad said at last. "Did you get the pony settled in, Jennifer? Is everything all right?"

"No problem," I said quickly. "She's fine."

I didn't want anybody to know how nervous I was about caring for Melissa. She hadn't looked big at the riding stable at home. Now that I had her to myself, all alone, she looked enormous. I'd always wanted a pony of my own, ever since I could remember. But a golden dream pony racing across an open field with its mane and tail flowing in the wind was one thing; a real, tired pony in a cow barn in the rain was another. Especially since there was no one for her to depend on but me.

Melissa belonged to the riding stable where I took lessons once a week. Mr. Scott, who owned the stable and gave lessons, took care of the horses and ponies himself. Some of the other riders and I helped out whenever we had the chance. We were a long way from being experts, but we helped to clean stalls and learned how to put on saddles and bridles and how to brush the horses and ponies and clean out their feet. Probably we were more in the way than anything, but it was fun, and sometimes Mr. Scott would give us extra lessons for our help.

I was too short for basketball, and though I was a pretty good softball pitcher, I was terrible at catching the ball if anyone hit it or threw it to me. I wasn't exactly what anybody would call a valuable addition to a team. Running around carrying balls and towels for other players wasn't any fun, either, and managing teams bored me to death. What I liked best was riding, and I did as much of it as I could.

We had started trotting our ponies over low crossrails in our classes and Mr. Scott promised he'd soon start teaching me to jump bigger jumps. Mom and Dad had said I could have more riding lessons after school was over, and the whole summer floated ahead like a golden promise, full of ponies and riding.

Mom illustrated books for young children. Sketches of rabbits for the book she was working on were pinned all over the walls of her studio. She was behind schedule because of unexpected school projects, and car pools, but an uninterrupted summer would give her time to catch up and have the book finished by fall.

Dad was busy with the complicated things he did with computers. He came home one evening when I was flopped on the living room couch, writing a book report on *Black Beauty* and trying not to get tearful, as I usually did, over the scene in the middle when Black Beauty talks to Ginger.

"I've been asked by the company to go to Texas," he said, looking pleased, as Mom came into the room.

"There's trouble with some of the new computers, and they want me to take courses to help solve the problems. Do you think you two could manage without me for a while?"

Mom assured him that I'd be spending most of the summer with the ponies, and she'd be at her drawing board, and that everything would be perfectly okay.

And all our wonderful summer plans *would* have been okay, if it hadn't been for the zoning board of our town.

Somehow, almost overnight, the board switched everything around and voted to let a condominium get built on the one pretty piece of land still left in the town— the apple orchard just across the road from our house.

There were furious meetings and angry letters to the local paper, but they did no good at all. The bulldozers sneaked in and ripped out the lovely old trees. Soon the pink and white blossoms that made the trees look like popcorn balls were gone, and there was nothing but mud under the huge wheels of the trucks. Tires screamed and motors shrieked just across the road from our house, and then the mud dried and the dust came, seeping under closed windows and driving us crazy every time we opened a door.

Mom kept the curtains closed at the windows of the room where she worked at her drawing board, trying to shut out the noise and the dust and the sight of the unhappy land. An old school friend of hers, Grace Browning, came to visit one weekend, stared at the mess outside our house, and quickly offered to lend us her summer place in Connecticut.

"This is impossible," she said to Mom. "I'm going to

Greece for the summer with a group of students from the school where I teach. I won't be using the house up there until after Labor Day. John won't be here—he'll be miles away from all this, in Texas. Why should you be stuck in this chaos when you could be working in the peace and quiet of a New England summer?"

Mom glowed with happiness at the idea. The problem, though, was me. Mom could draw her little rabbits for her book in uninterrupted tranquillity, Dad could be happy chasing glitches all over Texas, but what was to be done with me?

For a while there was talk of sending me away to camp. I had gone one year, and I'd hated it. The horses and ponies had been overworked and thin, and two of the ponies nearly died because the fences fell down and the ponies ran out onto a busy highway. I knew there were good riding camps somewhere, but I'd been so miserable I didn't want to try again.

"So what *do* you want to do?" Mom asked me as she threw the last of the camp catalogs into the wastebasket. "I'm really sorry. I don't want to be selfish, but I don't think I can bear to stay here all summer long. It's all such a dreadful mess of confusion where they're building, and so sad—it would be lovely to get away from it. And Grace's house looks so nice in the pictures she showed us. . . ."

So naturally I said I'd go with her, and tried to think of what I could do up there in the wilds of the country, alone, without getting hysterical with boredom. Dad suggested helpfully that I could read a lot, and Mom thought it would be nice if I took a little sketchbook and

8

practiced drawing, in case I wanted to be an artist one day.

I said something stupid to the effect that I had no intention of spending my adult life drawing rabbits in pajamas. This got me a stiff lecture from Dad and a lot of hurt feelings from Mom. I felt terrible, because she was really good at what she did.

I crept miserably out of the house to give everybody a chance to calm down. A friend of Mom's was driving by and gave me a ride to the stable in her car, and so I found myself in a stall weeping into the mane of a mostly black pony I'd never even seen before.

‹ 3 ›

She wasn't much of a pony, but she was comforting. I stopped feeling sorry for myself and went to get a brush. All the other horses and ponies were out; I could hear hoofbeats and voices as a lesson went on in the ring.

I had the stable and the black pony all to myself. She had a wide white blaze on her head and high white stocking markings on her legs.

I spent almost an hour brushing her off and combing out her mane and tail and making disapproving noises to myself over the condition of her feet. Of course, she couldn't have been here in the stable more than a day, or I'd have seen her before. Mr. Scott would be waiting for the blacksmith to come to trim her hoofs before she was ridden, which would be why she wasn't out working in the ring with the others.

I felt a lot better by the time the lesson was over and Mr. Scott came back into the stable. I guess my face was still blotchy from crying, though, because Mr. Scott asked me what was the matter. I put the patient pony away, sat down on a bale of hay outside her stall, and told him about my problems in a great rush.

"And all I wanted to do was ride this summer, and help with the ponies," I said, struggling to keep from crying again.

Mr. Scott listened thoughtfully, but he didn't say much. All the kids brought their horses and ponies into the stable just then and suddenly there was a lot to be done.

I got a lift home with a friend. Her mother dropped me off at the corner because our street had been closed off as a temporary parking lot for bulldozers. They were quiet now. It was late afternoon and all the workmen had gone home. The machines squatted out there in the twilight like monsters and I hurried by them, pretending not to see them, hating them and not liking myself much, either. None of this was my parents' fault and I'd acted like a spoiled brat.

I was terrific that night at dinner. I didn't say one single word about the long, boring summer waiting ahead for me. I made myself smile until my face ached as Mom and Dad talked excitedly about the little house in the country. I helped with the dishes and told Mom and Dad I was sorry for what I'd said, and went upstairs to wash my hair, feeling better about myself but not any better about the summer.

When I heard the phone ring, my hair was piled with suds on top of my head and the shower was running, so I paid no attention. By the time I'd blown my long hair dry and gotten dressed and gone downstairs again, my whole summer had changed without my having known a thing about it.

It was Mr. Scott who had called. And now he was there, right in our living room, talking to my parents. After I had said a surprised "hello," I curled up in the corner of the couch to listen.

"I'm sorry," my father was saying, "but we really can't afford a pony for Jennifer, much as we'd like to. Ponies are so expensive to keep. . . ."

I nodded sadly. I'd tried to work it all out one day in study hall at school when I was supposed to be doing my math homework. Boarding and shoeing and routine vet care. Blankets and a saddle and a bridle and halter. Buckets and a feed tub. Brushes. Hoofpicks. . . . The list was endless.

"It's hard," Mr. Scott agreed. "I know. I've been in the horse business all my life, and it gets tougher all the time. Feed and bedding prices today—" He shook his head. "But that's why I'm here."

Mom gave everybody fresh coffee and I sat sipping a glass of orange juice and not tasting anything until everyone had settled down again.

"I didn't come here to try to sell you a pony," Mr. Scott said. "Jennifer told me this afternoon about your plans to spend the summer in Connecticut and I know that particular area well. I worked up there as a boy. There used to be a lot of farming there and some pretty nice horses, too. A lot of open land and good fenced pasture. I came to ask you, if there's a fenced field near where you're going to stay, if you would let Jennifer take a pony up with you for the summer."

We all stared at him in surprise.

Poor Mr. Scott. He must have thought we didn't like the idea, because nobody said anything.

"It's the black pony you were grooming this afternoon," he said to me. "And I'd send along the feed and equipment you'd need, but you wouldn't really need much. Not just for the summer, with the pony out to grass."

He looked at my astonished parents. "This is a good pony," he said quickly. "I've known her for years. I've bought and sold her more than once myself. She's been shown some, and pony-clubbed a lot. She's got a bit of mileage on her now and she's not fancy enough for most people these days. I recognized her at a cheap auction last week, and I didn't like the looks of the characters that were bidding for her. The last thing in the world I need right now is another pony to feed, but I bought her again, anyway."

He shrugged his shoulders. "Just seeing her there, in that rotten place, after all those good years she's given to so many people—it didn't seem right. A good pony deserves better than what she was getting into."

He sat up straighter in his chair. "So now I've got a pony I don't need and, what's more, no place to keep her, once summer comes. I've got two horses due in as boarders, so I won't have stall room for this pony until fall. You'd be doing both the pony and me a favor if you'd take her along with you for the summer. And I think Jennifer would enjoy having her."

He looked at my parents questioningly and then looked at me. "She's a kind pony," he said, almost apologetically. "A little plain, but a really good kid's pony. She's had a number of different names in her time, but I've always called her Melissa. . . ." His voice trailed off again.

Then everybody spoke at once. "It's quite a responsibility," Dad said, just as Mom said, "Perhaps if we could work it out . . . ." and I said a jumble of words of excitement. A pony to care for and to have all mine, just mine, at least for a while? How could there be any question at all?

"It would be lovely for Jennifer," Mom said, looking dreamy. Mom herself didn't like getting close to horses, but she'd read an awful lot about them, and I knew she was imagining wild stallions racing across the plains with mountains and clouds and wind, and brave children taming wild horses in the wilderness—after all, even she'd seen the *Black Stallion* movie three times. And she knew *National Velvet* practically by heart.

I had to smile at her, and she laughed and jumped to her feet. "I think it's a splendid idea," she said. "Thank you, Mr. Scott. At least we'll see what we can do. I'm going to call the owner of the house right now and ask her."

Dad was asking Mr. Scott a bundle of questions as Mom and I rushed for the phone in the kitchen.

Mom got through to Miss Browning in a few minutes, and the news was wonderful. Her little house had once been a farmhouse and there was not only a fenced pasture behind the house, but an old cow barn, as well. A local farmer had built a nice stall in it and kept the last of his retired horses there for years. The old horse had died last fall and so there was an empty, snug stall, in good condition, right next to the house. Of course it would be nice, she said, to have a pony there for me.

Mom and I reported what she'd said. Dad smiled and gave up and said he had no more questions. It all sounded reasonable enough to him, if we took into account that we were out of our minds to take on such a responsibility.

When I went to bed that night my head was spinning with excitement. I watched the moon float past my window and finally fell asleep with the hoofs of moon-silver ponies galloping through my dreams.

< 4 >

"Oh," Mom said with a groan, adding "salt brick" to the list of things we'd need to take for the pony. "This is almost as bad as the lists we had to make getting you ready to go to camp."

I leaned over her shoulder. "*Two* lead ropes," I said. "One to lose and one to find. *Nobody* ever has enough lead ropes."

Mom changed the number to two. "What about shoes?" she said. "Maybe your father was right, after all. There *is* a lot to this pony business, just keeping track of everything."

"Melissa won't need shoes," I said quickly. "Mr. Scott said so. He said he'd have her feet trimmed again by the blacksmith just before we left. No shoes. Lots of ponies don't need them, if their hoofs are kept properly trimmed, because their feet are tougher than horses' hoofs, mostly."

"Right. No shoes." Mom pushed the list away from her a little and put down her pencil.

"That's not so much stuff, really," I said in what I

hoped was an encouraging voice. "You should see the check-off list for show horses they print in horse magazines sometimes. It would make ten more pages of things, at least. Baby oil. Hoof oil. Blankets and coolers and fly sheets and bandages . . . ."

Mom looked alarmed.

"Boots and bandages to protect legs and tails," I said quickly. "Things like thread for braiding, and darning needles for the thread, and clipping machines and soaps and polishes—"

"Okay." Mom laughed. "I'll take your word for it."

"Rain sheets," I went on enthusiastically. "Exercise boots and bell boots, girths and side reins, surcingles and extra bits, and stirrup leathers . . . ."

"I don't even know what half those things are," Mom said, getting up with a smile. "I'll settle for what we've got."

I could hardly believe my good luck. I spent every minute I could at the stable, making sure I knew how to do most of the things I'd always taken for granted. I practiced putting bridles on horses and ponies until I could almost do it with my eyes closed, and even learned how to take a bridle apart and put it back together again, which was a lot trickier than I thought it would be.

I bought two fresh, snowy white lead ropes for my very own out of my allowance, and a hoof pick with a bright red handle. Mr. Scott gave me a grooming box with some brushes and a currycomb and a sponge. We talked about feeding and watering and how much and

17

when, and I groomed Melissa every chance I got. Her winter coat was shedding and I loved seeing how her black coat shone, close and sleek, under the last of the heavy, longer hair that I brushed into little heaps on the ground.

Mr. Scott used her for some of the regular lessons, and gave me my lessons on her whenever he got the chance. Melissa went patiently around and around in the ring, only yawning a little from boredom sometimes as we walked and trotted and cantered and I began to feel comfortable on her back.

One afternoon, during a sudden shower of rain that delayed a lesson, Mr. Scott showed me a picture he'd found in his collection of horse magazines. It was of Melissa, looking bright and pretty, with her mane and tail neatly braided, at a show a few years ago.

"Nice little mare," Mr. Scott said. "She's taught a lot of youngsters in her time. I bought her out of an auction when she was a five-year-old and sold her as a first pony to a boy who's gone on now to ride show jumpers. I bought Melissa back from him when he outgrew her and sold her to some clients whose little girl had just started to ride. They never did think much of the pony. Wasn't elegant enough for them. So they sold her back to me and bought a fancy young Thoroughbred, instead."

He shook his head. "The new horse gave their daughter such a fright that she gave up riding. They wanted to buy Melissa back again, but somebody else already owned her by then and she wasn't for sale. At any price."

He put the magazine back on the shelf in the tack

18

room. "She's had other owners since then and I lost track of her. What a lot of stories these good ponies could tell, if they could only talk."

The spring shower had stopped and the horses and ponies were waiting with their riders. Someone else was on Melissa. I tried to feel forgiving. It wasn't my lesson day.

"I know you'd like to spend some time with the pony this afternoon," Mr. Scott said understandingly, "but she's got to pay for her keep while she's here. It won't be long before you have her all to yourself."

I was trying to concentrate on final exams, Mom was packing up her drawing things, and Dad was busy getting ready to go to Texas. Somehow, in the middle of all this, not one of us stopped to wonder how we were going to take the pony with us.

"Good heavens," Mom said, looking pale. "Mr. Scott just called and said he'd managed to borrow a station wagon and horse trailer for us. He wondered if we knew how to drive it."

"There you are," Dad said. "It's impossible. You'll have to give up the idea, Jennifer. I knew a pony would cause too many problems."

"I'll cope," Mom said. "I can learn. At least I can try. I'm sure it can't be too difficult; I've seen women driving horse trailers on the highway quite often. A car full of children and a trailer full of ponies—might be quite a lot of fun."

She wouldn't let me come with her when she took the borrowed wagon and empty trailer out for the first time.

Mr. Scott went along to teach her how to manage while I stayed in the stable and worried with Melissa.

Half an hour later I heard the trailer coming back. When I heard Mom's quick, light step at the doorway, I knew things had gone well.

"Piece of cake," she said triumphantly. "It's one of those things that looks harder than it really is."

She drove the trailer out again, alone. This time she was gone for almost two hours and even Mr. Scott was looking nervous by the time she got back. But Mom was smiling and looking pleased with herself.

"I took it through the center of town," she said, "to get used to traffic lights and such. It's hard to make a right turn, though, especially at first, so I had to keep turning left until I got the hang of it."

Mr. Scott showed Mom and me how the trailer hitch fastened, and how to check the electric wires that worked the lights and trailer brakes. Mom and I hooked it up several times, just to make sure we understood it all, and then Mom announced she was going to back the trailer out of the way beside the stable.

I shouted and waved my arms, trying to help, as the trailer zigzagged all over the stable yard.

"I feel like Alice in Wonderland," Mom said helplessly after her fourth try. "When you try to go backwards, everything works the wrong way."

After the fifth try we both started to laugh, and Mom ended up laughing so hard at herself that she couldn't see where she was going and had to stop and wipe off her sunglasses.

Mr. Scott gave Mom instructions for what seemed the hundredth time—even he was laughing—and all of a sudden, Mom got the hang of it and tucked the trailer into its parking place almost in a straight line.

"How did it go?" Dad asked that evening.

"No trouble at all, really," Mom said. And then she winked at me. "Piece of cake."

‹ 5 ›

"Remember now, the trailer will handle a little heavier with the pony in it," Mr. Scott told Mom as I helped him lift the back ramp into place and fasten it shut behind Melissa.

Mom nodded without speaking. With her hair tied back with a blue bandanna, and dressed, as I was, in jeans and a plaid shirt and sneakers, she hardly looked old enough to have a driver's license, let alone to be driving a horse trailer out on the highway.

I knew she was nervous. Her hands were sweaty—she kept wiping them quickly on her jeans, hoping no one would notice.

We all got into the station wagon. Mom was behind the steering wheel, trying to look as though she did this kind of thing every day, with Dad on the front seat beside her getting maps out of a briefcase. I sat on the middle seat, looking past the jumble of bags and boxes of our belongings through the back window of the wagon, and through the little window at the front of the trailer. I could see Melissa's head and I could watch her tugging hay from the net that was hung where she could reach it.

Mr. Scott made a last check of the trailer hitch and safety chain, made sure the trailer doors were tightly latched, and came back for a final word with Mom.

"This pony's traveled a lot of miles in her day," he said. "She shouldn't give you any trouble. Just take it easy the first few miles so she can find her footing. Then you can go a little faster."

"Right." Mom put on her dark glasses, took a deep breath, and started the engine. We moved gently out of the stable drive.

There were a few alarming thumps as Melissa moved in the trailer to get her balance. Mom's knuckles turned white as she gripped the steering wheel. But once we reached the main highway, the thumping stopped and there was no sound but the peaceful rush of wind at the car windows and the hum of the tires on the smooth surface of the road.

Mom relaxed her death grip on the steering wheel, Dad smiled and began to rattle the maps as he unfolded them, and I put my chin on my arms on the back seat of the car and watched Melissa eat hay as the miles went by.

Of course, Mom had never driven anything but a plain passenger car before, and from years of habit she got into the wrong lane at the first toll station.

"You're driving what's considered to be a truck," Dad reminded her as he looked up from his maps at the last minute. "It's a different toll in a different lane if you have more than four wheels—or is it the number of axles they count?"

Mom looked wild for a moment, and braked a little too quickly. Melissa's hoofs thundered around in the trailer, but she stayed on her feet. A few cars honked their horns impatiently, but the truck drivers beside us and behind us knew at once what was happening. They slowed and moved out of the way and the driver to the right grinned and waved and let Mom move over to the correct lane. He gave Mom the thumbs-up sign; she smiled and waved back gratefully.

Melissa gave a loud, long whinny as Mom stopped to pay the toll and this made us all jump, including the toll collector, who nearly dropped the change. Mom almost stalled the car as she turned around to look at me anxiously. I didn't know anything more than she did about ponies in trailers, but Melissa seemed perfectly calm, only curious, as she looked out the little side window and chewed cheerfully on her hay. She whinnied at every toll we went through, but we were ready for it the next time.

We didn't dare stop for lunch. Mom confessed she was afraid she wasn't ready to handle the trailer in a parking lot, especially if she had to back and turn it. The country around us opened into wide fields and gently rolling hills and woods, and Dad finally said, "Next exit—and turn to the right."

Mom let out a little sigh of relief. She slowed and moved down the exit ramp as smoothly as though she'd done it every day of her life.

"Nicely done," Dad said.

Mom smiled at me in the rear-view mirror. "It's not difficult," she said. "Just takes a little practice. You ought to try it sometime. It's fun."

The roads narrowed. Tree branches scraped against the sides of the trailer, making sounds like fingernails on a blackboard. I kept holding my breath, thinking Melissa would panic. Mom shuddered and Dad dropped his maps on the floor and we all waited, terrified, for the pony to start plunging around in the trailer from fear.

But we were the only ones who were worried about it. Melissa paid no attention. It was clear she'd done a lot more of this than we had.

"Next left, and look for a red mailbox," Dad said in a strangled kind of voice. I think we all felt by then that we'd been on the road for a hundred years. But the red mailbox was where it was supposed to be, and we soon had turned and were bumping gently down the drive. Bunches of leaves swished on the sides of the trailer, there were a few more screeches of branches on the roof, and then the driveway opened up to a wide area between a small white house and a streaky red barn.

"We're here." Mom turned off the engine, set the hand brake, and sagged against the back of the car seat. "I may never drive another inch, but we made it."

"You were super," I told her as I stumbled stiffly out of the car.

"Congratulations. You should be proud of yourself." Dad patted Mom on the knee and we left her to recover as we went to lower the ramp and introduce Melissa to our new summer home.

‹ 6 ›

It rained all night and all the next day, but no one cared.
Mom and Dad sorted things out in the house and I fixed
things up in the barn, hammering nails to hang the pitch-
fork and rake, and a row of extra ones for the halter and
lead ropes. Melissa watched over the lower half of her
stall door while I carried bales of shavings and feed into
the barn from the trailer between showers.

Even though I hadn't had a chance to ride her yet,
now everything had calmed down, it was beginning to
feel wonderful having Melissa all to myself. There was
nobody to rush her off for a lesson, no one to interrupt me
as I tidied her stall and brushed her until her black coat
shone almost blue in the dim, rainy light.

Tired and contented, we all went to bed early that
night. The next morning the sun was shining—it was a
super beautiful day to go riding.

I did all the routine chores, gave Melissa her breakfast, had breakfast myself, and fussed around for a while
getting things ready. It was almost the middle of the
morning before I put Melissa's bridle on—and discovered I'd forgotten to bring her saddle.

I stood in the sunlight staring at Melissa's bare back. I could picture exactly where I'd left the saddle—right inside Mr. Scott's stable door, where I'd put it down because somebody needed help with a pony that didn't want to be bridled. The pony'd had more sense than the rider, who was trying to get the bit in backwards, so I'd shown her how to do it correctly—and forgotten about the saddle.

Melissa turned her head and blinked at me curiously. Her back looked a long way up. It also looked very bare and very slippery.

How *could* I have done such a dumb thing as to have forgotten the saddle? I sat down despairingly on an overturned bucket. Could Mr. Scott send me a saddle, like cookies in a box to a summer camp?

Even if he could, it would take forever to get here. And what was I to do? Lead Melissa around like a puppy on a leash while I waited?

I stood up, furious with myself. Other people rode bareback. Indians had ridden bareback for years and years. Rodeo cowboys rode bucking horses bareback. Certainly I should be able to stay on a pony in a quiet field without making such a big thing of it. I put the reins over Melissa's head, pulled the bucket closer, climbed on it, and flung myself onto the pony's back.

Melissa waited. I sat up and shuddered. Quickly I buried my hands in her thick mane. The pony moved forward at a gentle walk, and I was sure I was going to tip over and slide off.

I clutched at the reins and Melissa stopped. I patted her neck and she turned her head and gently nuzzled the toe of my sneaker. I glanced down—the ground looked very far away. I looked up at Melissa's black ears instead, and pressed my heels against her warm, round sides.

The pony walked quietly through the open gate into the back pasture while I struggled to keep my balance. Gradually I began to be aware of other things around me. Yellow butterflies flickered across the pasture grass and a blue jay shrieked from the woods. The scent of crushed grass rose from Melissa's hoofs and the sunlight shimmered around us. Melissa blew softly through her nostrils and her bit made cheerful, chinking sounds.

A small breeze lifted her forelock and blew a piece of her mane over to the wrong side of her neck. Without stopping to think, I reached forward and smoothed the stray lock over where it belonged and realized, with a surge of joy, that I hadn't yet fallen off.

Time ticked by in sunny gold light. And by the time the morning was over, Melissa and I together had walked over all the pasture. I practiced turning her, and stopping. I was hot, tired, and triumphant. Even without a saddle, I no longer felt altogether like a helpless passenger—I felt I was riding again.

Mom took Dad out with the station wagon and trailer and taught him how to manage it. He drove it home to Mr. Scott and then went on his way to Texas.

There was a small pickup truck in the storage shed for Mom to use. It took us into town to do errands and the marketing, which was all we needed it for. Totally content, Mom went to work at her drawing board and I spent my days with Melissa.

The pale leaves in the woods began to darken to the

deeper greens of summer. I practiced riding in the pasture until I could trot and canter and gallop on Melissa without feeling every minute as though I were about to fall off. It was, I decided after a particularly successful morning, kind of like learning to ride a bicycle. Once I found my balance riding bareback and stopped worrying all the time, it was hard to remember how difficult it had seemed at the beginning.

The next morning we went outside the pasture.

There was a gate at the back, and a cart track leading invitingly across the next field. As we topped the hill, the countryside rolled away before us in patterns of pale pastures and darker woods. I could see the faraway roofs of houses and barns, and little dots of black and white cows sprinkled over some of the pastures.

Five deer stood near the woods at the edge of the field, watching us serenely with dark, gentle eyes. I quickly stopped Melissa—I didn't want to frighten them—but we must have looked like part of the countryside, because the deer calmly nibbled at the grass tips and paid us little attention.

The dappled shadows under an enormous old oak broke into pieces and became twin fawns that skipped out into the sunny field to join their mother. Melissa snorted softly with surprise—she hadn't seen them, either. The pale, creamy spots on their brown coats had made them almost invisible until they moved away from the dancing shadows under the trees.

I whispered softly to Melissa so she wouldn't move. The two tiny fawns raced in bobbing little circles, stopping occasionally beside their mother. She nuzzled them

and licked them as they nursed, and then they would spin away from her again in their bouncing game of tag.

The sun was high and the day was getting hotter. I reached down to brush a fly from Melissa's shoulder, and when I looked up again, the deer were gone. They had faded into the woods as silently as smoke. I stared into the shadows unbelievingly, but all the deer had vanished. Melissa tossed her head and moved restlessly. I patted her on her shining neck and we went on.

Melissa and I explored the field and finally turned toward home. Another cart track ran beside a tumbled wall, and Melissa jogged along it quietly. I was thinking idly of ways to make her mane lie smoothly on one side of her neck as we reached a place where the ragged wall was replaced by a high, strong, rail fence. I wondered if this meant horses. Most of the farmers used wire fencing for their cows; this kind was different. We came to a wide, sturdy white gate and I pulled Melissa to a stop.

I sat up as straight as I could, trying to make myself taller, and looked into the field on the other side of the fence. The grass was a deeper, richer green there, as though it had been especially well cared for, but the ground sloped away, out of sight, not far beyond the gate, and there was nothing more to see.

Melissa tugged lightly at the bit and I let the reins slide through my fingers. She put her head down and started to eat some grass. I watched, and listened, but I could hear nothing but bird sounds in the woods.

"Come on, Mel," I said lazily. "Let's go on home."

I had started to shorten my reins when Melissa suddenly whirled and put her head over the gate, letting out a long, loud whinny. I clutched at her mane, tense with surprise. Melissa's head was high, and her black ears were straining forward. She whinnied again. She turned and gave a solid thump of her shoulder against the gate.

"*Melissa!*" I said wildly, trying to get the reins sorted out while I struggled to untangle them from her mane. The pony danced sideways and slammed her shoulder against the gate again.

I was certain she was going to mash my leg against the gate. I couldn't understand what was happening. I pulled my leg up high to try to keep it out of the way and gave Melissa a stinging slap on her neck.

"*Cut it out, Melissa!*" I roared at her. I'd never raised my voice to her before. It surprised her as much as it did me, and she stood still for a moment. I snatched up the reins.

With a shaky sigh of relief, I started to turn away from the gate. Melissa moved two polite strides toward home and then took a slippery little sideways step. I grabbed at her mane again, but it was too late. Melissa whirled and I slid off and landed in a furious heap on the ground. The pony tore the reins from my hand and I sat there, raging, as she put her tail high into the air, gave a buck and a kick, dashed down the track a few feet to where the fencing ended, and plunged into the woods. Without me.

She was hardly as graceful as the deer—I could hear her crashing merrily through the woods. At least this made her easy to follow. I stumbled after her.

< 7 >

"Come back here, Melissa!" I shouted into the woods. I knew very well she wouldn't pay any attention to me, but yelling was about the only thing I had left to do as I tripped and floundered through the thick underbrush.

I stopped. I couldn't hear a sound. Even the birds had been startled into silence. Maybe Melissa's bridle had been caught by a branch and she was waiting somewhere nearby for me to come rescue her.

Terrific. I hurried more hopefully along a narrow path until it led into a small open clearing.

No Melissa. Just some trampled grass beside some panels of rail fencing—the same kind of fencing I'd seen beside the gate out in the field.

The top rail was broken. I scrambled over the fence and tripped over Melissa's bridle lying on the other side, half-hidden in the grass. I scooped it up. Now, at least, I was sure she'd come this way.

I ran on through the thick, lush grass. The sun was hot and my sweaty jeans and shirt stuck to me all over, but I was too mad to care.

I reached the top of the rise. The ground sloped

sharply away in front of me. It was like standing on the rim of a wide, shallow bowl.

On the far side, a stream traced a thin silver thread across the green of the grass. Beyond the stream was a white gate and the roof line of a big house, partly screened by trees. There were other low, small white buildings to one side.

All of this must have registered in my mind somehow, because I remembered it later, but all I could see just then was a herd of spectacularly beautiful ponies whirling around the black and white pattern of pony that was my Melissa.

I started to run down the hill toward the jumble of ponies. I could hear neighing and the flurry of spinning hoofs. There were tossing manes and tails, the glint of shining eyes, and the twinkle of white markings as the ponies swirled around Melissa.

I looked toward the house for signs of help, but everything there was still.

The kicking and fussing stopped. A small white pony, with its ears back and teeth flashing, drove the others away from Melissa.

Melissa trotted away a few strides and stopped. She wasn't limping—from where I was, still running, she didn't look hurt at all. She shook her black head until her mane stood on end, and pawed the ground.

I stood still for a minute because I had to, catching my breath and waiting impatiently for the stitch in my side to go away. If Melissa needed rescuing, I sure didn't know how to do it.

I sat down and tried to breathe more slowly, and as I

watched, wondering what to do, a milky gray pony, the color of pond ice in winter, came from one side in a long-strided, floating trot. His long mane and tail were white and there were white dapples on his sides and hind-quarters. With his neck arched and his mane and tail flowing as he moved, he circled the other ponies and stopped.

For a moment there was silence, and then, in a great rush, all the ponies started running together, with Melissa joyfully in the middle. Ponies of different colors swept past me on the hill as though I were no more than a shadow in the grass. There were flashes of sunlight on coppery chestnut shoulders, a spark of red from the flanks of a bay—gleaming brown heads and the ripple of grays, white stars and flashing white fetlocks, all flying across the pasture grass.

I jumped to my feet and stared after them. I didn't have the least idea what to do.

The ponies turned and slowed, and their wild gallop was over as quickly as it had started. They made their way to the banks of the stream. A few of them drank and all of them scattered and began grazing peacefully.

I looked again toward the house. No angry owner had appeared, shouting for me to get my pony out of there—no signs of life anywhere. Maybe, if I was very lucky, I could capture Melissa and sneak out of the pasture with-out anyone knowing we'd been there at all.

I hid the bridle behind my back and moved toward the grazing ponies. A pretty little chestnut with a narrow white blaze came over to greet me. A gray pony followed her, and then a bay—I could easily have caught any of them. The only problem was that it was Melissa I was after, and she wanted no part of me.

She dodged away from my outstretched hand whenever I got anywhere near her. I was getting so desperate I was starting to grab for her mane, which only made things worse. She liked being where she was, in the company of all those beautiful ponies, and it was clear she was planning to stay.

I was hot, tired, and furious. I went back up the hill and sat down near the broken fence, glaring from a distance at Melissa. I flopped back on the warm, sunny grass and closed my eyes, wondering what to try next. Squirrels chattered in the woods behind me, crickets chirped in the grass beside me, all of them sounding disgustingly cheerful. I listened to them for a while until their sounds drifted and faded—I fell asleep.

I woke up with goose bumps all over my arms and itching everywhere. The sun was low in the sky and the deep shadows of the woods had reached out into the field; the warmth had gone from the afternoon.

I sat up quickly. The ponies were still grazing quietly. I sorted out the jumble of straps of the bridle I still held in my hand and got to my feet to try to catch Melissa again.

It was late. Ponies, I knew, liked patterns in their lives. Melissa was used to coming in for her evening feed. Maybe, if I pretended it was all regular routine, I could fool her into letting me catch her this time.

I marched down the hill as though I did this every day. "Come on, Melissa," I said in a firm voice. "Time to go home."

The other ponies watched as I went right up to Melissa. I fished the stub of a wilted carrot from the pocket of my jeans. Melissa reached forward, took the carrot gently from my hand, and stood meekly while I slipped the reins over her head and put the bridle on.

I hung onto the reins as though they were a lifeline to tomorrow. The other ponies crowded around us curiously. "I'll bring all of you some carrots. Another day," I promised them, pushing them gently out of the way. I tightened the throatlatch of the bridle another hole in case Melissa changed her mind and tried to slip away, but she followed along willingly as I led her to the broken fence. I tugged the reins lightly, she jumped the lower rail, and I borrowed a low rail from another part of the fence to shove into the gap where the top rail had been broken.

The other ponies watched from the hill. The ice-gray pony trotted in a circle, whinnied once, and led the ponies back down toward the stream.

I hung fiercely onto Melissa's reins. I was terrified she'd want to go with them. She did whinny once, but softly, and made no more fuss as I started to lead her toward the narrow path in the woods. She was ready to go home.

< 8 >

I was stiff and sore the next morning. Melissa looked a little weary, too, so I didn't go riding. I turned her out into the pasture for the day and I went grocery shopping with Mom.

I was embarrassed that I'd fallen off, so I hadn't told Mom the whole story, but I did tell her about seeing the field full of beautiful ponies. She asked the owner of the market about them as he helped us carry the grocery bags to the pickup truck.

"Oh, sure," he said. "Those are Mrs. MacIntyre's ponies over at Hidden Valley Farm. She's raised show ponies for years, just as her father did. She has a big place down in Virginia, but she grew up here, and she brings some of her ponies with her when she comes back to stay every summer. Says it's cooler here and the change is good for the mares.

"The ponies have been at the farm for a few weeks now, but the main house isn't open yet. Her regular caretaker got sick—a boy from one of the local farms stops by there twice a day to check the ponies. Not that they can come to much harm where they are, can they?

39

Fencing's good, plenty of first-class pasture, and the stream there for water. I know the place well. My dad used to hay those fields before he retired a few years back."

"Does Mrs. MacIntyre have children who ride the ponies?" Mom asked.

"No. No kids. Hers are grown and gone. The ponies she brings up here generally aren't the riding ponies, anyway. The ponies your daughter saw would be the mares turned out with her new pony stallion. She paid some record price for him last winter and flew him over to this country. She bought him in Wales, I think. Nice-looking pony. They ran his picture and a story about him in the local paper."

He shut the door of the truck and squinted up at the sky. It was a brassy blue and the leaves were limp on the trees. "We're in for a spell of hot weather. It'll be good for the early hay."

The heat may have been good for the hay, but it wasn't much good for riding. Melissa would get shiny with sweat just grazing in the pasture. Inside the cow barn it stayed dim and cool, though, so I began keeping her in her stall during the day and turning her out in her pasture at night.

I got up very early during the heat wave and rode while the morning mists were still in the fields. The soft, smoky silver blurred the edges of the fields and woods, and until the mists burned away in the sunlight, it would feel as though there were no one else in the sweet summer mornings but Melissa and me. I stayed well away from the pony pasture. I didn't want to go through all that again.

Sometimes we shared the early mornings with the deer. Once we surprised them as Melissa trotted over the crest of a hill. I didn't know deer ever made sounds of any kind, but there was suddenly a funny, harsh whistle. Melissa snorted wildly and shied. I fell off, but this time I held onto the reins.

The loud whistling sound came again. One of the tallest deer was standing facing us, stiff legged, almost out of sight in the mist. As Melissa and I both stared at her in astonishment, she stamped one foreleg sharply, whistled again, and whirled to follow the others into the woods.

Melissa was still shaking with fright. I didn't blame her. I'd been as startled as she was.

Usually the deer drifted silently into the underbrush if we came on them suddenly in the woods. There was seldom so much as a ripple of leaves to tell where they'd left the path. But now and then the peculiar whistle would come blasting at us, sometimes in the woods and sometimes in the fields, and this never failed to send Melissa into a dive of fright.

It was very hard to stay on when she moved so fast and unexpectedly. If I didn't actually go off, I'd end up draped over the back of her neck near her ears, or snatching at her mane as I tried to stay on. It was a most undignified performance at best. I'd always thought of deer as sweet, shy, timid creatures, yet they sent me over

Melissa's violently shying shoulder, hurtling into the bushes at the side of the path, more times than I liked to admit, even to myself.

It took me a while, but gradually I learned to sit straight and shorten my reins—something, I realized guiltily, Mr. Scott had been trying to teach me at home. It hadn't seemed important enough then, but at last I was learning.

Melissa and I spent hours every day out in the woods and fields. We jumped tiny fallen logs and then bigger ones. Fat and friendly stone walls welcomed us to jump them, though I had to be careful to make sure no boulders had spilled from their tops to hide in the grass, where Melissa might take off or land on one.

The grass in the fields grew tall. It shimmered and rippled around us. Blazing white daisies and dark-gold black-eyed Susans sprinkled the fields like fallen stars. Sometimes Melissa and I would gallop and seemingly jump forever in the fresh mornings. Other days I'd put a sandwich in the pocket of my jeans and we'd wander quietly through the countryside, stopping in a shady spot near a stream to let Melissa drink and rest and dream her pony dreams while we listened to the low murmur of the water as it spilled over the mossy stones.

Once in a while we'd find ourselves near the gate to the pony pasture. I could handle Melissa much better by now. If she fussed and danced at the gate, I could stop her and make her behave herself. When she whinnied, the herd of shining ponies would come tearing up the pasture hill like gangbusters.

The ponies would slide to a stop at the gate and I

would give them carrots, if I had any in my pockets, and pat their pretty heads as they gently nuzzled my hands. The ice-gray pony would stay to one side, nostrils flaring, and watch me with glowing dark eyes from under the cascade of his white forelock.

After a few minutes he would march over to the gate, accept one piece of carrot, and spin away again. The other ponies would follow, racing away with their manes and tails flying.

Poor Melissa. She would dance at the ends of the reins and call after them sadly. She couldn't understand why I wouldn't unlock the gate and ride in with the other ponies. There was no way I could tell her we would not be welcome in somebody else's pasture full of ponies, much as I had begun to wish we could join them, too.

The heat wave broke. A crashing bunch of thunder-storms came boiling over the pasture hill. By the next morning, the steamy, heavy heat was gone and the green woods and fields looked as though they'd been freshly washed and then dipped in silver and gold. The crystal-bright sky was dotted with small, fat white clouds that stood out against the blue like the dapples on the ice-gray pony.

Melissa's eyes sparkled and she pounded on the stall door as she waited for me to take her out that morning. She fussed impatiently while I put her bridle on, and pranced as we trotted across the pasture. She chinked the bit, and tiny white flecks of foam dotted the toes of my sneakers.

Melissa swung toward the pony-pasture gate and we

stopped. She whinnied loudly. There were no ponies in sight, but we heard them answer, and the whole herd came winging up over the crest of the hill.

They were too full of joy in the bright morning to stop. They galloped past the gate with their dark eyes flashing and their hoofs thundering on the soft ground.

Melissa put her head over the gate as far as she could to watch them go by, and called after them. She pawed sharply at the gate—both of us longed to be on the other side.

Without stopping to think, without giving myself a chance to change my mind, I spun Melissa away from the gate. She leaped into a canter, almost as though she knew what I had in mind. We followed the pasture fence until it ended at the corner, and turned into the woods.

‹9›

The narrow trail was almost invisible. Bushes and trees were thick with summer leaves, and branches dipped across the path. The green light was dim and shimmery, almost like being underwater—even the birds I could hear in the trees, high above us, seemed to be making watery sounds as they sang.

I ducked against Melissa's shoulder, kept my head down, and closed my eyes, letting the pony find her own way. I felt branches pull the fasteners from my hair and slide across the back of my shirt. Eventually Melissa stopped. I sat up, blinking; we were standing in the sun-lit opening in the woods, beside the spot where Melissa had broken the rail fence before.

With a shiver of excitement I jumped off, slipped the top rail, and led Melissa into the pony pasture.

I jammed the top rail back into place and swung up onto Melissa's back. The wide green valley curved away from us. Melissa threw her head high and I looked up to see the herd of ponies moving restlessly near the wide white gate where they'd seen us last.

"Come on, Melissa!" I shouted, and loosened my reins.

The ponies whirled at the sound of my voice and came racing toward us. Melissa galloped to meet them.

We were riding in a whirlwind of bay ponies and chestnuts, grays and brown and blacks. Manes and tails flew like banners in the wind—there were flashing eyes and forelocks blowing back, and dark, shining hoofs skimming over the summer grass like swallows in the sun. Time stood still.

I felt my hair streaming behind me, the sun and the wind in my face, and Melissa's powerful stride as she raced with the other ponies—

The ponies circled and slowed. Their nostrils were flaring and light sweat darkened their necks and flanks. The dappled pony sailed around us once more at a trot and then stopped. The other ponies settled into a walk, some of them tossing their heads as though they, like me, wished they could have galloped on forever.

Even Melissa, fit as she was, was puffing a little, and all the ponies walked quietly together, catching their breaths as they made their way down the slope to the stream.

They sipped the bright water, swishing their muzzles and playing with the ripples. A chestnut pony splashed a shower of water high into the air with her hoof, while a bay pony went down to roll in a shallow spot, jumping to her feet streaming muddy water, with a fern frond caught in her forelock.

The ponies moved away from the stream, drifting out into the pasture and lowering their heads to graze.

I glanced nervously toward the house. I saw no one running toward the pasture gate near the house to chase me away, but I felt guilty, anyway. Melissa and I had finally done what we'd wanted to do, and it had been as much fun as I'd thought it would be, but I didn't want to push my luck. Shaking my hair back from my face, I pressed Melissa into a canter.

There was a hollow in the pasture, high on the hill near the fence, out of sight of the house. I looked back over my shoulder and felt like the Pied Piper—all the ponies were trotting after me. I stopped Melissa and got off, and the ponies crowded around me.

Gentle muzzles poked at the pockets of my jeans, and friendly dark eyes gleamed at me from under wind-tossed forelocks. I shared pieces of carrots with them all, giving an extra piece to the small white mare that seemed to be their leader, and to the ice-gray pony waiting, watching silently, a few steps to one side.

Melissa had her share, and the carrots were quickly gone.

Giving the chestnut pony with the white blaze a last pat, I led Melissa to the fence. All the ponies watched with their small ears pricked.

"Go away," I said to them. None of them moved. My legs were tired from hanging onto Melissa's sleek back during our wild ride, so I sat down on the grass and waited. Melissa stood at the end of the reins, half-dreaming in the sunlight. Gradually, just as I'd hoped, the ponies lost interest and turned away to graze.

I hurried Melissa over to the fence and took down the

top rail as quietly as I could. The last thing in the world I needed was for the whole gang of ponies to rush to the fence to follow me while I had it down. I clucked softly to Melissa, she hopped over the low rail, and with a huge sigh of relief, I tucked the top rail back into place.

I struggled onto Melissa as quickly as I could and urged her into the woods. I heard one pony whinny in a questioning kind of way, but Melissa didn't answer, and we were soon out of sight. The glowing green leaves closed around us and we made our way home.

‹ 10 ›

A few days later, one of the far fields was mown and everywhere the air was sweet with the fragrance of new hay.

I sat quietly on Melissa's back at the edge of the field as twilight turned the sky to dark velvet. The deer we'd been watching had melted into the deepening shadows and were gone.

I turned Melissa and started back across the pasture while there was still light enough left for us to see. She blew softly through her nostrils and waggled her ears, dipping her head now and then to nip off the head of a daisy that glowed in the last of the sunset.

In this part of the pasture the daisies were high. I stopped Melissa, leaned over, and picked three of them. I tucked them into her brow band just behind her ear. Melissa tossed her bit lightly and moved forward again with the daisies in her bridle shining and bobbing with each step.

When we reached the barn I propped a flashlight on a beam in the stall and groomed Melissa with long, lazy strokes of the brush. By the time I'd finished, the stars had misted over and a puffy breeze was clicking the catches on the stable doors. It felt and smelled like rain, so I gave Melissa an armful of hay, freshened her water bucket, and shut her in the stall for the night.

I was glad I did. The next morning the gray rain was falling in wild sheets, blown by a heavy wind. The sturdy little cow on the weather vane on top of the barn danced and spun. The rain fell and the wind blew for three solid days, and by the time the storm was over, Melissa and I were so tired of doing nothing that we felt ready to explode.

The morning after the storm blew away was bright and warm. I gave Melissa a little grain and turned her out into her pasture before breakfast, and she went bucking and kicking across the field, glad to be free of her confining stall after so many days.

By the time I'd had my own breakfast and went out to catch her, she was mud and grass stains all over from rolling joyfully in the field, celebrating her fresh freedom.

I tidied her up as well as I could, put on her bridle, and we swung across the pasture in the welcome sunlight.

I was as tired as she was of looking at walls. I'd made cookies, which were good, and a cake, which didn't rise properly but tasted okay, read, and tried not to bother Mom. She was trying to get the colors right for the jacket of the rabbit book. She mixed her paints over and over again, but the colors all looked dreary in the storm's dim light from the rain-streaked window beside her drawing board.

We'd even gone to a movie one afternoon, which had

bored us both. The windows and the roof had leaked in the pickup truck, which somehow seemed funny. We'd laughed all the way home and ended up having a good day, in spite of ourselves. But all of us were very glad to see the sunlight again.

Some poor farmer had baled the hay in a far field just before the storm, and the soggy bales lay in pitiful lumps in the short, wet grass. I wondered if the hay in the rained-on bales would ever be any good for livestock to eat, but Melissa and I discovered they made marvelous jumps. We spun around the hot, bright field, sailing over the hay bales, until both of us were breathless and happy.

I walked Melissa into the cool woods along a familiar path. The storm had blown several huge branches down which were too tangled and leafy for us to jump, and in one place, a whole tree had fallen. We had to leave the path several times. She and I battled through the woods, turning and following the thin little deer trails that laced through the thick underbrush, until we found ourselves in a forest of pines where we'd never been before.

Melissa's hoofs made no sound at all on the thick carpet of pale brown pine needles that had fallen to the forest floor. No direct rays of sun could shine through the pines and the light was dim and shimmery.

Melissa stopped and pawed curiously at the pine needles under her feet. We heard the sharp call of a pheasant from far away and the sound was thin, as though it had been sifted through the trees. I shivered a little and shortened my reins.

"Time to go home," I said briskly to Melissa. She turned obediently at the touch of a rein and then I pulled her up again. There was no sign of a path—not even a faint deer path—showing anywhere. I had no idea what direction we'd come from—I was completely, totally, absolutely lost.

I pressed my heels against Melissa's sides and she moved into a brisk trot. But when we reached the edge of the pines, there was nothing ahead of us but thick, unbroken woods. Still no sign of a path.

I spun Melissa around and she broke into a fidgety canter. Back through the silent pines on silent needles— ahead of us was a stone wall, jagged and tall, with more heavy woods behind it.

I pulled Melissa up sharply and she skidded a little on the slippery needles. I dropped one hand and pressed it apologetically on her shoulder. I wondered why the more lost I felt, the faster I wanted to ride. It didn't make any sense at all, and I was getting Melissa all sweaty with anxiety for no reason.

I made myself sit still until the pony and I both calmed down. "Okay," I said out loud, to Melissa's questioning ears. "Ponies are supposed to be clever. Take me home, Melissa."

I'd read somewhere that horses and ponies had a trust-worthy sense of direction. Like many lost dogs and cats, they could find their way home if they were given the chance. I giggled a little nervously. As far as I knew, we could have been in Zanzibar, though I wasn't even sure where Zanzibar was, either.

I clucked softly to Melissa and loosened the reins. She took two or three uncertain steps forward as though ask-ing me what she was supposed to do. I made sure not to move my hands or legs to guide her and I clucked to her again.

This time she swung sharply to the left and walked forward determinedly. We made our way through the fragrant, shaggy pines. I ducked under a few low branches I was sure I'd never seen before. More than once I wanted to stop Melissa and change direction because I saw a shadow or the bent trunk of a tree I thought I recognized. I even pulled her up once, but the silence pressed around us, the dark pines stood in sullen stillness, and I shivered again and quickly let her walk on.

The pines ended. A leafy path appeared in the woods ahead of us. Melissa broke into a trot, splashing joyfully through puddles left by the storm. They bounced back blue light, reflecting the sky shining through the thinning woods, and we cantered out into an open field.

It was a weird feeling, as though Melissa were being led by an invisible string. She turned to the right, and as we topped the crest of the hill and cantered through a gap in a stone wall, I could see ahead of us the white buildings of a farm, the field full of the hay bales we'd jumped, and our own house and barn beyond it.

I gave a shaky laugh and patted Melissa gratefully. She knew I was pleased with her, even if she didn't know why. It didn't matter—we jogged in relieved and friendly silence toward home.

‹ 11 ›

The moon was a slip of silent silver behind the thick tops of the trees. A smudge of pale daylight glowed beyond the pasture hill.

I leaned sleepily on the window sill of my room, watching the moon set and wondering what had made me wake up. I heard a dog barking from the distance and the bubbling sound of an owl in the woods. But I was used to all these night noises and I heard nothing strange.

I yawned and blinked my blurry eyes. The faint breeze of very early morning came in my window, bringing the deep, sweet smell of the far, freshly hayed fields. It rustled the leaves of the oak trees near the house, but this was a familiar sound, too.

I yawned again and was turning to go back to bed when the breeze died and I heard a light tapping sound, and a clink from the far side of Melissa's pasture.

This woke me up completely. I looked beyond the dark shape of the barn to the far side of the field. I could see the blotchy white markings of Melissa out by the back gate. And I knew from the sound that Melissa was trying to undo the gate latch and let herself out of the pasture.

Ponies. I'd learned what escape artists they could be. Melissa had let herself out of her stall twice until I'd gotten smart and put a bolt where she couldn't reach it. The pasture-gate latch near the barn was even easier for her to open, so I'd soon learned to tie a rope around it to keep the gate shut. But I'd never thought to tie the gate on the far side of the field.

I groaned and grabbed for my clothes. I was hopping on one foot tying my sneaker laces when I heard a last click as the latch opened, and a grating sound as Melissa shoved the gate open and trotted through it.

I pulled on a sweater and ran across the hall to the door of Mom's room. I tapped on it quickly.

I opened the door a crack and poked my head in. "Melissa's gotten out of the pasture," I said.

I heard the sheets rustle as Mom sat up in bed. "Do you want me to come help catch her?" she said.

"No, thanks, that's okay," I said. "I'm pretty sure I know where she's going and it isn't far. It's almost daylight, so there won't be any problems. I just wanted to tell you I was going after her in case you woke up and I wasn't here. Go back to sleep."

Mom murmured "Good luck" after I'd promised to come right back if I couldn't find the pony. I shut the door softly and hurried down the stairs, through the kitchen, and out into the fresh morning.

Bridle. Where had I left it? I couldn't remember. But Melissa's halter and lead rope were hanging near the pasture gate. I snatched them off the post, ducked through the rails, and ran across the field.

It wasn't until I was halfway across the pasture that I slowed down to catch my breath. There was no reason to rush. Melissa probably had gone to visit the other ponies at the pasture gate. Maybe she'd get in with the ponies again, but she could come to no harm romping around with them as she'd done before. I'd heard at the post office one day with Mom that Mrs. MacIntyre had sent her staff up to open the house; she was probably there herself by now. But if anyone did see the ponies charging around the big pasture, I'd just catch Melissa—as soon as I could—say I was sorry, and remember to tie the back gate shut the next time.

I walked more slowly. I hadn't thought to bring a flashlight, and it was still quite dark in the shallow hollows of the fields. The grass was wet with dew and swished around my sneakers.

Swinging the halter and rope in my hand and humming under my breath, I made the last turn in the track and was frozen into sudden stillness when I saw the patchy black and white shape of Melissa half hidden in a thick clump of overgrown blueberry bushes. She hadn't gone all the way to the pony field gate, after all. I spoke to her very softly—I didn't want to startle her. Something was wrong.

I could see the white blaze on her face as she turned her head toward me and gave a low, nervous nicker of greeting. I went up to her quietly. I wondered if she'd gotten hurt somehow—I couldn't understand what was the matter.

I slipped the halter over her head, snapped on the lead rope, and gave her a crumbling lump of sugar from my pocket.

Melissa swung her head sharply toward the pony pasture. Her head was high, and as I put my hand on her shoulder I could feel her shaking. Her ears were pricked in the direction of the gate and I turned to see what it was that had made her so anxious.

There still wasn't a lot of daylight, but I could just make out the dark shape of a truck standing silently by the gate.

I heard voices then. Men's voices, speaking in low tones.

"Get some kind of lights on," I heard one of them say. "Parking lights will do. Tom's got to find his way back when he gets hold of those ponies."

The parking lights went on like sparks in the darkness. The dawn wind suddenly felt cold, and I shivered and pressed against Melissa. My sneakers squished, wet with the dew, if I moved. I stood very still. I hoped Melissa would, too.

I peered frantically through the leafy branches of the tangled blueberry bushes. Melissa flung her head still higher as the faint, pale shape of a pony came into sight. I was just able to tell it was the smallest white pony mare. There was a rope around her neck, and I could make out the silhouette of a man leading her.

"Got the leader," he said. "The others are following right along, just as I told you they would."

"There's not much size to that pony," another man said. "The horses we picked up in New Jersey last week were a lot taller."

"Sure," said the first man. "But those were out of a cheap riding stable and they were thin. These ponies are in great shape. I came up here to check them out, and I told you—they're carrying good weight."

"Hurry it up," another voice said. "We haven't got much more time. It'll be full daylight soon."

Melissa drew in a deep breath and I thought she was going to whinny as we heard the hoofbeats of the other ponies trotting up the hill. I clung fiercely to her muzzle, and all she could manage were a few little muffled sounds that could hardly be heard, certainly not above the rising sound of hoofbeats as the other ponies topped the rise and came toward the gateway where the truck was parked.

I heard the thumping sound of hoofs on a loading ramp. "Get out there behind the others," I heard someone say. "These ponies are tame enough. It should be easy to herd the whole bunch into the truck."

I let out my breath in a silent gasp. I hadn't realized I'd been holding it so long, and my ears were starting to ring. In the gradually growing daylight I saw the shapes of the ponies, turning their heads uneasily as two men walked behind them. But the little white mare was already inside the truck and, though a few of the ponies hesitated, most of them walked right up the ramp.

The dappled gray stallion with his snowy white mane

and tail made a pale blur as he spun in a circle. He was easy to see in the dim light. Two ponies broke away from the herd and raced out of sight, down the hill—I couldn't tell which ones they were—but the stallion wouldn't leave. He raced back and forth, sliding to a stop, rearing and turning, and finally, with one last despairing whinny, he plunged up the ramp to be with his mares. I could hear his hollow hoofbeats from inside the truck.

"Good enough." I heard the quick creak of the ramp being lifted and the harsh grating sound of metal bolts sliding shut. "Come on. Let's get out of here." The three men, who were still no more than dark shapes in the early morning light, swung into the cab of the truck. The engine ground into life, the truck shuddered a little and began to move forward slowly. It turned to follow the track down toward the road.

The truck lurched and swayed on the uneven track. I watched, stunned, until the red taillights vanished.

‹ 12 ›

I was terrified. I didn't know what to do. How could I stop a truck with three men in it? Throw myself in front of the wheels and yell for help? There was no one to hear me, anyway, out here in the back fields.

Chase after it on Melissa until it got to the highway? Joke. What good would that do? I couldn't reach out and stop it, even if Melissa could catch up with it.

What I needed to do was ride for help.

I dragged Melissa out of the blueberry bushes and flung myself on her back. I pressed my heels against her sides and she plunged into a gallop. Through the open gate into the pony field, across the top of the hill and down toward the stream on the far side of the pasture— she ran as though she had wings on her hoofs.

The sun had risen and flames of gold tipped the tops of the trees. There was plenty of light and the stream stretched ahead of us, looking a lot wider than it had ever seemed before. I clung to Melissa's mane. The stream ...llow. I thought she would gallop through it. But ...t instead.

...she almost made it. But one

hind hoof slipped as she took off, and she couldn't quite make it all the way to the other side.

Water flew around us. Melissa stumbled forward onto her knees. I sat as still as I could, trying not to go off, clinging desperately to her mane as she struggled to keep her balance. The water wasn't terribly deep—just about up to her knees—but it splashed around us and held her legs, and the rocky bed of the stream was uneven and covered with round, slippery stones.

The pony snorted and blew wildly through her nostrils as she flung herself high into the air and then forward again. We reached the far side in a series of wild plunges and Melissa half-scrambled, half-jumped up the muddy bank.

She almost fell again, but somehow she found her footing in the sliding mud. And somehow I stayed on. She gave one last enormous leap forward. At last there was firm grass under her feet again, the stream was safely behind us, and ahead stood the tall white gate that led to the house and to help for the stolen ponies.

I sat up straight on Melissa's back and tugged at the halter rope to slow her. I would unlatch the gate and ride through it, or climb over it and run up to the house on foot—but not according to Melissa. She shook her head, tossing her black forelock, and tiny drops of stream water scattered like diamonds over her ears. She galloped on.

The huge white gate shone in the light of the rising sun. Melissa raised her head a little, checked her stride, lengthened it again, and soared over the gate.

There was smooth grass under us again and then blue-gray crushed gravel sprayed from under her hoofs as we

reached the driveway. There were no lights on at the back of the house. I spun Melissa to the right and we galloped along the drive to the front entrance.

She skidded to a stop. I flung myself off her back. There was a flight of steps leading up to the porch and to the front door—I couldn't possibly reach it unless I took her with me.

"Come on, Melissa," I said in a strangled kind of voice. She hesitated, arching her neck and snorting suspiciously at the steps. I gave the lead rope a desperate tug, she plunged forward bravely, and her hoofs thundered beside me as we raced up the steps and across the wide porch to the front door. I pounded on the door with both fists—I was too out of breath to shout. I found a bell in the shadows and pushed it over and over again.

I was making so much noise myself that I didn't hear any footsteps, but the door swung open at last.

"Quick, quick," I said in a gasp to the dim figure of a woman in a bathrobe, standing at the opened door. "Somebody's stolen your ponies. Call the police."

Lights went on all through the house. Doors opened, half-dressed people rushed in and out of rooms. I heard the sound of a telephone and, above all the confusion, the quiet voice of a woman asking for the police.

I put my arms around Melissa's neck and leaned against her wet shoulder. My head was spinning. So much had been happening in such a short time—

Two people came to the door. They asked me questions. What color was the truck? How many men? Had I seen the license plate?

66

I answered the best I could. I'd tried to see the license, but there was so little light, and it was mostly covered with mud. . . . I thought it had been white, with black numbers, but I couldn't be sure—

Melissa and I waited. I heard a car start and then another, and they barreled down the driveway toward the road.

I heard the cool, firm voice of the woman who'd first come to the door. "Ask Anne to come take this poor child's pony," she said.

My hands clamped more tightly than ever on the soggy white lead rope. *Nobody* was going to take Melissa from me. But then a tall, pretty girl with dark hair, dressed in riding clothes, came around the corner of the house.

"I'm Anne, Mrs. MacIntyre's niece," she said as she came up the porch steps. "I'm helping with the ponies for the summer. Let me take your pony for you."

I looked at her and shook my head in silence. My hands were still holding Melissa's lead rope so tightly that they were aching. No one was going to take Melissa out of my sight.

<　13　>

Anne reached out to pat Melissa. The pony turned her head and rubbed it against the sleeve of her pale yellow shirt, leaving streaks of mud on it. But Anne didn't seem to mind.

"They need you inside the house," she said gently. "I promise I'll take good care of your pony. As soon as you're done, you can come to the stables to see her. After I've got her cooled off and comfortable, I'll put her in one of the pony stalls."

I looked at Melissa again. She was breathing fast from our wild gallop, and even under all the mud and the water from the stream, she was still sweating. Anne was right. Melissa should be walked until she stopped puffing.

I hesitated for another moment. Anne waited, stroking Melissa's shoulder. "Okay," I said at last, and handed her the end of the lead rope.

With a nod, Anne turned the pony and coaxed her down the porch steps. I watched until they disappeared around the corner of the house.

Someone told me to come into the house, and I did, and stood dripping muddy water onto the flowered carpet in the front hall. My knees felt funny, but I didn't want to sit down on the cream-colored cushions of the chairs in the hall in my soggy jeans.

A man asked me to tell my whole story again, repeating everything I'd heard the men say as they loaded the ponies onto the truck. I shut my eyes and told him everything I could remember.

"You poor child." A young woman in a gray dress with a white apron came hurrying down the hall toward me with a smile, tucking the last wisps of hair under a small pleated cap. "Come with me. They'll soon find the ponies—Mrs. MacIntyre's already called the local police, and she's speaking to the State Police right now—"

Chattering cheerfully, she led me down the hall. Before I knew what was happening, my wet, muddy clothes were gone, I was wrapped in the folds of a thick, furry pink bathrobe that was miles and miles too big for me, and I was sitting in a steamy, bright kitchen staring at a blueberry muffin on a plate in front of me.

It stared back at me with dark, unblinking blueberry eyes.

"I think I should call my mother," I said in a shaky voice.

There was a phone in the kitchen, and I called Mom. She said she'd be right over, and she was. She rushed into the kitchen, gave me a warm hug, and vanished into the main part of the house to find out if there was any news.

She was back in a few minutes with a shake of her head. "No word of them yet," she said, "but the State Police are here and they want to talk to you."

I got numbly to my feet, scooped up the folds of the pink bathrobe as well as I could, and trailed along behind Mom into the living room across the hall.

I told my story again. The State troopers, huge in their uniforms, disappeared. I caught a glimpse of flashing lights outside the windows and heard a siren starting as they went off down the drive.

"How do you do, young lady." The older woman who had opened the door—how long ago was it? I'd lost all track of time—stood in front of me and stretched out her hand to me. She wasn't even pretending to smile and I was grateful. There sure was nothing to smile about. "I am Mrs. MacIntyre. Come and sit down and let me thank you for coming so quickly."

Mrs. MacIntyre and Mom and I sat near a bay window and I looked at the flowering plants there in the brightening sunlight while Mom and Mrs. MacIntyre talked in strained voices.

A silver tray appeared with coffee and tea and cocoa and a basket of fresh muffins. Mom had a cup of coffee and dashed home to get me some dry clothes. Mrs. MacIntyre went to talk on the telephone again. I watched my cocoa turn cold and poked at it with a spoon.

As soon as Mom came back and I was in my own dry clothes again, I went to find Melissa.

There was a paved courtyard between two wings of the low, white stable. Tubs of yellow and white flowers stood on each side of the doorway and bloomed in boxes under the windows. Inside, the stable was full of morning sunlight, shining on the dark paneling of the stalls and turning the polished brass to gold.

Melissa heard me coming; she put her head over the lower part of her stall door and nickered soft sounds of welcome as I went to her.

I rubbed her ears and smoothed her forelock. She was fresh and clean; there wasn't a trace of our wild ride on her anywhere. Even her mane and tail had been washed and brushed out. Her stall was bedded in sweet, deep straw, and a shining yellow bucket, filled to the brim with water, was within easy reach, just inside the stall door. I put my face in her mane for a moment and I couldn't help smiling. Whatever else was happening, I certainly didn't have to worry just then about Melissa.

Anne came down the stable aisle and we left Melissa to go back to her hay. We went outside and sat together on a white bench near the stable door.

"There's a telephone in the tack room," Anne said. "If there's any news, they'll call us from the house. You must feel you've told your story a hundred times this morning, but I still haven't heard exactly what happened. Could you bear to tell it again?"

< 14 >

I told her everything, starting with Melissa letting herself out of the back gate of the pasture. I thanked her for taking such good care of Melissa and she said she'd been glad to have something to do—she'd wanted to go help look for the ponies, but Mrs. MacIntyre wanted her to stay nearby so she could go to them if they needed her when they were found.

We talked about the ponies and Anne told me all about the ice-gray stallion. "He's beautiful, isn't he?" she said. "He's a Welsh pony and his name is Ash Grove. My aunt has wanted him for *years*, and she finally got the chance to buy him a few months ago."

After a few minutes I wiggled forward on the bench. "Tell me," I said. "Nobody else will. I know it's terrible the ponies were stolen, but they'll be all right, won't they? What can the thieves do with them, anyway, except sell them at an auction or try to sell them to riding stables somewhere? Then they'd be recognized—ponies that beautiful don't just come out of nowhere."

Anne stared silently at the toes of her gleaming short boots. "It's the killers that scare us," she said in a low voice. "It's a matter of finding them before the ponies are taken to a packing house. It's hard to identify anybody's horse or pony once it's turned into frozen meat."

There was an awful silence. I didn't know what to say.

"It sounds like a bad movie on television, doesn't it?" Anne said. "But there's been more and more of this— horses and ponies being stolen right out of stables and from pastures and fields. There's a huge demand for horse meat and the price is high—that's why horse-stealing is growing so."

Her voice faded and she kicked at a pebble near the bench. "Those poor ponies," she said in a whisper. "They must be so frightened and confused—"

I jumped to my feet. I didn't want to picture those lovely ponies jammed together in the dark, dirty truck, being driven to their sad and ugly destination.

Anne got up, too. "I'm going to bring those last two ponies into the stable," she said fiercely. "I can't bear to think of them still out there in the pasture where we can't see them every minute. I know the upper gate has been shut and the gardener has put a chain and a padlock on it, but I want those ponies *in*."

She got two halters and lead shanks from the stable, and a measure of grain, and we went together to catch the ponies.

I shuddered when we reached the enormous white gate to the pasture. It was hard to imagine I'd jumped anything that big on Melissa, though her hoofprints were plain on both sides of it.

The two young ponies didn't want to come in. "They're only four-year-olds," Anne said, starting to laugh as they whirled and danced, just out of reach. "They really should be broken by now, but my aunt decided to let them each have a foal by Ash Grove this year." The chestnut pony, with the four neat little white socks and narrow blaze on her pretty head, dipped her muzzle into the grain measure and Anne captured her quietly.

The other, a little bay with a white star on her forehead, stopped playing and followed us to the gate. Anne handed me the halter. I slipped it over the bay's head and we led the two ponies to the stable.

We cross-tied them in the aisle as Melissa watched from her stall. Anne showed me where the grooming things were kept, and we started to brush the ponies. It was good to have something to do.

Tiny particles of dust floated in the air and turned into sparks of light in the sun streaming through the windows. It was comforting to have the brush in my hands and to hear the soft swishing of the bristles as we worked. The smooth, glossy coats of the ponies turned to satin. Their fine, shining manes and tails rippled like water as we brushed every strand. We cleaned their small hoofs and even polished them—still no word from the main house.

"That really is enough," Anne said at last, putting down the hoof oil and pushing her hair away from her hot face. We shut the two ponies safely in the stalls near Melissa. Anne took me on a tour of the stables and tack room, I gave Melissa some grain because she'd missed her breakfast, and I was leaning on her door, watching her eat, when the telephone rang in the tack room.

Anne raced to answer it. In a minute she was at the door again.

"They've found the ponies," she said, her voice shaking with excitement. "The police stopped the truck just this side of the state line. They *were* on their way to a packing plant. Can you *imagine* how terrible this could have been. . . ." She sprinted toward the main house and I ran beside her.

‹ 15 ›

Ponies, ponies everywhere. The courtyard was full of them. The green truck stood in the driveway with its battered ramp down. The inside of the truck was dark and ugly and looked like a big mouth ready to swallow the ponies and carry them off again. It was a relief when the police came, put up the ramp, and drove the dreadful thing away.

Mrs. MacIntyre was in the center of the courtyard. The ponies swirled around her and she reached out to touch each one, calling them all by name. There were tears of joy in her eyes and for a little while she spoke to no one but the ponies.

Anne gave me a handful of lead ropes. Working together, we slipped a rope over each pony's neck and, one by one, sorted them out and put them into the stable. Some of them were bruised a little, the small white mare had a cut over one eye, and Ash Grove, who was the last one to come in, had a deep gash on one leg. Anne left me holding the tired stallion's lead rope while she went to call the vet.

"He'll be here right away," she said as she came back,

carrying a halter. She slipped it onto Ash Grove's head, patted him gently, and clipped the crossties to his halter.

Mom, who had been watching everything from the back lawn, came into the stable with Mrs. MacIntyre. As Anne put a temporary bandage on the stallion's injured leg, she and Mrs. MacIntyre discussed each pony in low voices while Mom and I kept out of the way and smiled at everyone and everything.

The vet came and each pony was brought out of its stall, checked thoroughly, and put back again. The cut over the eye of the little white mare was not serious. Only the cut on Ash Grove's leg needed stitches. I stood at his head and stroked his tiny ears the way Melissa liked best, and soon he was freshly bandaged. He was shivering a little, even though the day was warm, so Anne buckled a yellow and white stable sheet on him and put him away in a deeply bedded stall.

Anne and the vet went to check each pony for a second time. Mrs. MacIntyre took Mom and me back to the house, once we were sure all was well with the ponies. The police were waiting to talk to me again.

Finally they were done. Mrs. MacIntyre thanked them over and over, and it was wonderful to watch them drive away, slowly this time, with no lights flashing and no sirens screaming.

"Lunch!" said Mrs. MacIntyre with a smile, and I realized I was suddenly hungry. I glanced at the grandfather's clock ticking softly in the corner of the living room. Almost three o'clock—and I hadn't had any breakfast. It had been a long morning.

We had lunch on a terrace overlooking the wide, green

pony pasture. "It looks so sad and so empty without the ponies there," Mrs. MacIntyre said. "I don't think I could ever have come up here again if my ponies hadn't been found in time. At least I know they're safely in the stables, and I've already ordered new fencing put up, with an alarm system, that should discourage thieves in the future."

"It seems so hard to believe," Mom said. "Horse thieves in the twentieth century. . . ."

"They take dairy cows, calves, horses, ponies—anything they can get their hands on," said Mrs. MacIntyre. "Sometimes just one or two, sometimes half a herd or more. It seemed like a joke to a lot of people at first, when all this thieving started, but now the police know there are rings of thieves working through black-market packing plants all over the country. And they're making an incredible amount of money. . . ."

Her voice trailed off. We all sat in silence, looking out at the empty field.

"But at least I was more fortunate than many have been," Mrs. MacIntyre said in a more cheerful voice. She smiled at me. "Thanks to you and Melissa. You must have done a lot of riding to be able to jump the stream and the gate bareback the way you did."

"I didn't have an awful lot to do with it, once we started across your pasture," I confessed. "All I did was try to stay on. The rest of it was mostly Melissa."

We talked more happily about the ponies and had all kinds of sandwiches, and iced tea sprinkled with tiny pieces of oranges and lemons, frosted so cold that the glasses were misty.

I leaned back against the striped cushions of the chair. Mom and Mrs. MacIntyre sipped coffee and talked in quiet voices. I was warm and tired and contented and my mind drifted to the ponies safely in their stable, and to Melissa, waiting for me. . . .

"I think she's asleep," I heard Mrs. MacIntyre say softly, from what seemed a long way off.

"No, I'm not," I managed to say. "I've got to go get Melissa and ride her home—"

No chance. Mom was positive and so was Mrs. Mac-Intyre. I'd done enough for one day, and so had Melissa. She could stay in the stable until the next morning. I was not to worry about her. Anne would give her the best of care—

This woke me up because it was so funny. If I ever had anything to worry about, it wasn't going to be the kind of care that Mrs. MacIntyre and Anne gave to their ponies.

"Melissa probably thinks she's died and gone to heaven," I said with a laugh. Anne said she'd give Melissa an apple with her supper, and Mom and I went home.

I was late getting started the next morning. I overslept, and then decided to strip Melissa's stall and pile it up with deep, fresh bedding as a welcome home. Once this was done, I had to find my bridle. I looked in all kinds of weird places and finally found it where I'd put it, in the kitchen closet, waiting to get a thorough cleaning.

I soaped and polished it, and shined the bit so that Melissa would look pretty when we left Mrs. MacIntyre's stable. This took so long that it was almost noon by the time I hurried across Melissa's pasture, through the gate she'd opened at the back, and followed the cart track across the field toward the gate of the pony pasture.

My breath choked in my throat as I came over the rise and saw a truck near the pony gate again, and my hands went all sweaty before I saw it was not the sinister green truck this time. This was a huge flat-bed truck, loaded with bright rolls of chain link fencing—and there was a whole crew of men digging post holes next to the older rail fence. More men were standing near a panel truck, measuring distances and consulting each other as to where they were going to install the electronic alarm Mrs. MacIntyre had ordered.

I had to laugh, partly from relief because I'd had such a scare, and partly at Mrs. MacIntyre's determination. Her ponies were going to be protected, one way or another.

There was still room for me to get through where the old gate had been. I felt pretty strange walking past the men with a bridle in my hand, but I managed a light "Good morning!" and tried not to look like a horse thief as I half-ran across the pony pasture.

I crossed the stream where it was shallow and had stepping stones, ducked through the white gate, and went into the stable.

I'd been looking forward to talking to Anne, but there was no one there. Melissa called out to me with a loud whinny of greeting. I gave her the apple I'd brought for her and went down the stable aisles, looking at all the other ponies. They'd been washed and brushed and were edgy and restless, anxious to go out into their pasture again. Ash Grove put his head over his door. He'd had a bath, too, and though his legs were still thickly bandaged, he was his old sparkling self.

‹ 16 ›

A silky summer rain was falling as I trotted Melissa along the soft shoulder of the road the next day. It would have taken a tank or a helicopter to get into the Hidden Valley pony field by now. I didn't dare even ride up to the back pasture gate any more—I was afraid Melissa and I would set off the electronic alarm if I did.

I turned Melissa into the driveway and rode to the stable. I didn't want to be a nuisance, but I was anxious to know how the ponies were and to see them again.

I'd called and Anne had said of course I'd be welcome, and she was waiting at the stable door.

"You're soaking wet!" she said. "Come on in before you drown!"

"It's a nice rain to ride in," I said as I led Melissa into the stable. "Melissa and I don't shrink. Are all the ponies okay?"

"Most of them are fine," Anne said, throwing a yellow and white plaid cooler over Melissa's wet back. I borrowed a halter, cross-tied Melissa in the aisle and left her to steam warmly and to dry under the soft woolen cooler.

"Two of them are a little sore this morning, but the vet was just here and said they'll work out of it once they're turned out in the field again. I'll be keeping the white mare in for a while, and Ash Grove, of course."

We went down the aisle, stopping by each stall. It was fun to see each pony's name and breeding on a bright brass plate on the stall door. The small white mare was Hidden Valley Holly, and my particular favorite—the chestnut with the narrow white blaze—was her daughter. Her name was Hidden Valley Berry.

By the time we'd finished admiring all the ponies, the rain had stopped and the sky was brightening.

"I'm going to turn the ponies out now," said Anne. "Would you like to help?"

Of course I would—I loved being with the ponies. We put halters on them and led them, two by two, out to the pasture gate.

We slipped their halters off and watched them race away from us, bucking and kicking and delighting in their freedom again. All of them went out into the field except Ash Grove and Holly.

Melissa was waiting on the crossties. "She's such a sweet pony," Anne said, patting Melissa's shoulder. "I'd love to see you ride her. Would you like to jump over some of the fences in our schooling ring?"

She pulled the plaid cooler off Melissa, folded it, and hung it on a blanket rack. "We're going to bring a few of the young ponies up here next summer for me to work with," she said. "There was kind of a mix-up this spring, when the caretaker got sick and then the stable manager in Virginia had to go to England to get all the import papers straightened out for Ash Grove's flight to this country. Even after all that planning, the pony came over sooner than we'd thought he would. So instead of shipping him from the airport in New York all the way down to Virginia, and then vanning him back up to Connecticut with the mares, Mrs. MacIntyre had them all brought here a few weeks early."

She laughed and shook her head. "It was an absolute zoo for a while. We were all spinning in different directions."

She opened the gate for me and I rode Melissa into the ring.

"Don't you want to borrow a saddle?" Anne said. "I'm sure we have some that would fit you and Melissa."

I laughed. "I'm not sure I'd remember how to ride in a saddle any more," I said. "I've been riding bareback all summer. No, thanks, I'm fine."

It seemed strange to be riding in a ring again. I warmed Melissa up and let her look at the jumps, which were all scaled to pony height and decorated with white tubs full of yellow and white daisies.

"How big do you want the fences?" Anne asked. "I'll set them up for you."

"I have no idea," I said. "I never measured anything we jumped this summer. About as high as your hip, I guess—nothing as big as the pasture gate! One of those was plenty."

"That gate's over four feet high," said Anne. "Quite a jump for a pony. I think three feet will do nicely for your Melissa under ordinary circumstances."

Melissa and I had a wonderful time. We didn't need to worry about rough takeoffs or hidden stones and branches on the landing side of the jumps, as we did out in the fields. Melissa was jumping perfectly and we were sailing across the ring toward the in-and-out made of white rails when the reins suddenly felt strange in my hands. I shortened them, my eyes still on the approaching jump.

Melissa skimmed through it neatly. I straightened up, patted her on her shining neck, and said "Whoa" to her quietly. She settled back down to a walk.

It wasn't until I started to turn to ride back toward Anne that I saw the bridle had twisted and Melissa had no bit in her mouth.

"Darn it," I said. I stopped Melissa with another "Whoa" and jumped off. The cheekpiece of the bridle had slipped. The buckle had been crooked since the day Melissa'd unloaded me by the gate and broken into the field with the ponies, losing her bridle near the fence. I'd straightened the tongue of the buckle a few days later, when I noticed it wasn't right, and I'd paid no more attention to it.

Anne hurried anxiously across the ring. "You had me worried there for a minute," she said, reaching out to pat Melissa. "What a marvelous pony this is! Most of them would have run off, or spun around, or done all kinds of nutty things if their bridles broke like that."

I nodded absently, fiddling with the narrow straps of the bridle. "Melissa doesn't care. Not in a fenced ring, anyway. I'd bet she'd jump this whole course without any bridle at all."

Anne looked politely interested, but I saw she didn't really believe me.

"Here," she said, handing me a white lead rope. "You can put this around your pony's neck and hold her here. Let me have the bridle for a minute. I'll find a cheekpiece to fit and you can borrow it until yours can be mended."

I stood and waited beside Melissa. Maybe the MacIntyre ponies would get into trouble if *their* bridles broke in the ring, but then, they weren't Melissa.

She was bored. She pawed the sandy surface of the ring impatiently.

With sudden determination, I swung up on her back and turned her with a touch of my heel. She broke into a smooth, collected canter.

With nothing more than the soft cotton lead rope held loosely around her neck, I guided her with the shift of my weight and the light pressure of my heels against her sides. Melissa turned and galloped and jumped wherever I asked.

"So there," I said to her triumphantly as I straightened up and brought her back to a quiet walk.

"Lovely. Perfectly lovely."

I looked quickly over to the side of the ring and my face grew hot with embarrassment. I felt like a show-off, though I hadn't known anyone was watching me. I rode over to the gate and stopped and said "Good morning" to Mrs. MacIntyre.

"Do you usually ride your pony without a saddle *or* a bridle?" she asked.

I laughed and explained about the saddle I'd left behind, and the broken buckle on the bridle. I knew Melissa was wonderful, but she wasn't *that* wonderful—she could get quite fresh out in the open fields. And then there was always the unexpected to cope with. Like the whistling deer. I smiled and rubbed Melissa's ears. She knew I was proud of her.

As Anne came to the gate with the bridle, Mrs. MacIntyre said I would be welcome with Melissa at any time. "And please give my best to your mother," she said. I promised I would.

Mrs. MacIntyre went back to the house while Anne and I fussed with the new cheekpiece until it was right, and I got back on Melissa.

"Please come again," Anne said. "It's fun to have company. I sure wish I'd known you were up here all summer. We could have sent for another pony and we could have gone riding together. It's too late now, though. We're going back to Virginia this weekend. But next year—"

Next year. I thanked her, said good-by, and slowly rode down the driveway. I didn't want to think about next year—I didn't even want to think about next week. It was time for us to go home, too.

< 17 >

Dad drove the borrowed station wagon and the trailer up a few days later. He'd had an interesting time in Texas and we heard all about the crazy computers. It was great to see him again.

What wasn't great was packing up and putting things away. It was awful sweeping out the last of the bedding from the barn, stuffing the hay net, and loading Melissa onto the trailer for the trip home.

Mom and Dad chatted quietly as we drove on our way. I watched Melissa through the windows every minute, saying a silent good-by to our summer.

We stopped at Mr. Scott's stable near the ring. A lesson had just ended and the riders came rushing over, dancing around the trailer to welcome Melissa back and asking jumbles of questions. My hands felt stiff with sadness as Mom and I lowered the ramp. I went in to clip a lead rope onto Melissa's halter, and backed her gently from the trailer.

Mr. Scott came over, glowing with praise at how well Melissa looked. I said all the polite things I should and led Melissa to her stall.

A little girl with dark braids came up to me shyly. "I have an apple," she said. "Would you like to give it to your pony?"

"Why don't you give it to her yourself?" I said. "She's not my pony any more."

Our house smelled moldy from having been shut up all summer. The half-finished condominium across the street was hideous. I cried myself to sleep that night.

I went to see Melissa every chance I got, though it wasn't the same. She always knew me, of course. Even if she was trotting around the ring in the middle of a lesson, she'd whinny to me when she heard my voice.

I rode her in my own lessons and it felt funny and strange to ride her with a saddle again. I had to wear a hard black hunt cap, too—Mr. Scott wouldn't let me jump without one.

School had started. It was nice to see my friends again and to hear about their summers and what they'd done. But I'd stand in the school hall some mornings, with the sunlight blazing outside, smelling mops and dust and disinfectant, and wish I were out on Melissa chasing cloud shadows across the grass.

Anne called from Virginia. All the ponies had traveled well and were fine, Ash Grove's leg had healed and he'd won a Grand Championship somewhere important. Five men had been arrested for the theft, and three of them had gone to jail.

Melissa lost some of her brightness. She was okay, but she was quiet. Probably she missed the freedom of our summer, too.

"We got spoiled," I told her one rainy afternoon as I brushed her in the stable aisle. "We had too much fun, I guess."

But I wouldn't have changed a minute of it—even the times I'd fallen off, or the desperate ride in the dim morning light to save the stolen ponies. I made drawings of the deer in the mist for art class, and wondered if I'd ever see them, or the Hidden Valley ponies, again.

"Mrs. MacIntyre called this morning," Mom told me when I got home from school one afternoon.

"Really? Whatever for? That's great. How are the ponies?" I dumped my books on the kitchen table. My pencils scattered and fell to the floor and as I knelt to pick them up, their bright yellow color reminded me of the yellow and white flowers at the stables, and the plaid coolers hanging in the stable aisle.

My throat ached. Maybe I was getting the flu.

"You'd just left for school," Mom said. "She said she'd call you this evening."

I went upstairs to start my homework, but I couldn't concentrate, and I was the first to run to the phone when it finally rang after dinner.

"I'm pony poor," Mrs. MacIntyre said with a laugh. "I have all my lovely show ponies, and Ash Grove, and all the pony mares, but not a one for my own grandchildren to ride. I would like to buy Melissa."

At first I couldn't think of a word to say. "Whatever for?" I managed at last. "She's not at all fancy, nobody knows her breeding. Nobody even knows exactly where she came from. . . ."

"She's a good pony," Mrs. MacIntyre said. "And sometimes that can be the hardest kind of pony to find. I
started my own daughters on my show ponies that were
really too much for the girls to handle. They gave up
riding as soon as they could. It was a mistake I don't plan
to make again. When my grandchildren come to visit
me, I need a pony they can trust. A gentle pony that can
teach them what fun it is to ride."

"Melissa," I said. "Of course."

"I didn't want this to come as a complete surprise to
you," Mrs. MacIntyre said. "I've spoken to Mr. Scott.
But I didn't want you to feel I was taking the pony away
from you. . . ."

I closed my eyes. I could picture Melissa with all the
other beautiful ponies, snug in the stable or out in the
grassy green valley. Even if I never saw her again . . . .

Mrs. MacIntyre waited for me to say something. When
I didn't, she went on. "I know you will miss her, but the
pony will have a good home with me," she said. "And I
hope you can come up next summer to stay with us. You
and Anne could ride together, you would see Melissa, of
course, and you might enjoy helping Anne break some of
the young show ponies. . . ."

I'd see Ash Grove again, and all the pony mares with
their new foals next spring, all running together with
Melissa—

"Mrs. MacIntyre," I said at last, "I can't think of anything in the world more wonderful for Melissa. Or for
me. It's a super surprise."

I hesitated. It was time to share my own secret.
Melissa's shape was getting suspiciously round, even tak-

ing into account her thickening winter coat. I'd seen Mr. Scott give the pony a questioning look once or twice as we'd started out for a lesson. I was no pony expert, but I'd brushed and groomed and cared for Melissa long enough to know her well, and I'd started to wonder a little.

I'd told no one about the day Melissa had dumped me off and gotten into the field to run free with all the pony mares and Ash Grove.

I took a deep breath. "Mrs. MacIntyre," I said, "I think Melissa may have a surprise for you, too."